To Grandma Berndt, who inspired me to face each day
—M.B.

To Camp and Shaw, may your curiosities always lead
—B.L.

THE HERO WITHIN

Michael Berndt
Illustrated by Brad LeDuc

PUBLISHED BY:

Lowell Milken Center
FOR *Unsung Heroes*

I like school. As a matter of fact, I LOVE school! Where else can you hang out with your friends, travel to distant planets, and learn about ancient civilizations, all while getting exercise and proper nutrition? One of my favorite subjects in school is social studies. Our teacher, Mr. Dexter, has recently been teaching us about citizenship. I've learned all about how someone can become a citizen and the rights and responsibilities of a good citizen!

During one of our lessons, our class learned all about famous citizens. Some of these citizens are so special they have earned the right to be called heroes. We learned about Dr. Martin Luther King Jr., Amelia Earhart, as well as Abraham Lincoln. During the lesson, Mr. Dexter wrote the words, "UNSUNG HERO" on the board and asked if anyone knew what that meant. Carson, the class clown, raised his hand and said, "Oh, that's a superhero who can't sing!" Mr. Dexter smiled, said it was a good guess, and then told us the real definition.

We learned that an unsung hero is a person who has done something truly wonderful in the world, and has never really been fully recognized for it. He went on to say that these people are not the superheroes seen in movies or comic books, but real people that had the courage to make a positive difference in our world! What really surprised me was that Mr. Dexter said there are thousands of these incredible people who have never been truly discovered!

As the lesson went on, Mr. Dexter began giving examples of real unsung heroes who were unknown to us. He asked us if we had heard of Paul Revere. Of course we all knew that he was the man famous for riding through the night warning colonial townsmen and women of the approaching British. Mr. Dexter's next question stumped the class. He said, "Tell your neighbor who Sybil Ludington was." The classroom was quiet. We later learned that Sybil Ludington accomplished something just as amazing as Paul Revere! On April 26th, 1777, the 16 year old Sybil Ludington mounted her horse, Star, and rode all night in the cold rain to warn American colonists of a British Attack. I was even more amazed to learn that her ride was nearly twice as long as Paul Revere's!

My classmates and I were hooked, and we begged Mr. Dexter to tell us of another unsung hero. We then learned about a man named Adam Shoemaker who was a preacher and teacher in southern Indiana in the early 1820's. Mr. Shoemaker was very much against slavery and often taught and influenced his young students regarding his feelings about freedom and emancipation. Mr. Dexter stopped his story and told us that sometimes the work of unsung heroes can go unnoticed for a long time, yet the effects of their efforts can be timeless. Although at that time, we didn't quite know what he meant, it all made sense when Mr. Dexter revealed that one of Mr. Shoemaker's young students was none other than Abraham Lincoln.

The class was a buzz of conversation about what we just learned. The lesson ended with Mr. Dexter giving us all an assignment. Immediately, we could tell this was no ordinary assignment. We were given the task of going out and discovering a real unsung hero. We were to uncover our hero's story, create a presentation, and share his/her amazing feat! I was so excited to think that there were stories like the ones we learned in class, just waiting to be discovered. The best part is that I could be the one to uncover one of those stories and share it with the world!

Rushing home after school, I burst into the house and began working on my assignment. I decided to begin by looking up the official definition of 'Unsung Hero'. The definition I found stated that it is, "A person who makes a substantive yet unrecognized contribution; a person whose bravery is unknown or unacknowledged." That's where I hit a dead end. How was I supposed to find a hero that is unknown? At supper that night, I shared the events of the day with my family and told them all about the assignment. I also shared my frustration about finding a lead. My parents told me not to worry and assured me that they knew of just the right help I needed.

The next day, my grandparents came for a surprise visit! My grandmother sat me down and said that she had just the information to help me with my assignment. We talked about how hard it is to find a hero who hasn't been discovered. Grandma smiled and said, "Let me tell you a story." She began telling me about a little boy who grew up in the middle of World War II. He lived in a country called Lithuania, was torn from his home by the Nazis, and placed into a work camp with his family. Luckily for the little boy, he was bribed out of the camp and secretly hidden in another home near his community. Eventually, the Soviets liberated the camp and freed everyone.

Grandmother continued her story by telling me that the little boy was fortunate to later be reunited with his family. Seeking safety and refuge, his family embarked on a journey of nearly two thousand miles across Europe. Arriving in Nuremburg, Germany, an American stronghold, their freedom was finally secured. Convinced that America was the safest place to live, the little boy and his family gained a visa to travel to the United States. I was amazed to learn that after arriving in the U.S., the boy went to school for the very first time in his life.

I told Grandma that this little boy had an incredible story and was very brave. I still wasn't sure what made him an unsung hero. It was then that my grandmother told me how the boy's life turned out. Continuing her story, she told me that the boy grew up to enlist in the Army, work his way through the ranks, and become a decorated veteran in the Vietnam War. That wasn't where his story ended! Soon after serving in the war, he continued to be promoted and became one of the most influential leaders in developing the Green Berets in the Special Forces! He was even eventually promoted to Major General! Grandmother then reached in her purse, saying she had a picture of him to show me. As I examined the picture, I noticed there was a man in the picture shaking hands with former president Bill Clinton! As I took a second look, I noticed something familiar about the man in the picture. I looked at my grandmother and said, "Is that…?" Then grandmother said, "Yes, your grandfather was that little boy. He is quite a hero, although he really won't admit it."

Returning to school that next Monday, I couldn't wait to share with Mr. Dexter and the class that I had a real unsung hero in my family! Although my grandfather never rode a horse to warn of an invasion or taught a future president, he overcame many challenges early in life, never made excuses, and worked hard to be a leader. He made a difference. That's when I realized the assignment had two parts. Sure, we were supposed to search for an unsung hero and hopefully uncover a story to share with the world, but I think the second part of the assignment was to find the hidden potential within each of us. Knowing that my own relative was a true hero made me realize that these people are simply ordinary people that have the courage to do extraordinary things. I, too, have the responsibility to be a good citizen and take a stand to help make our world a better place. So now, I pass the assignment on to you!

**Lowell Milken
Center for
Unsung Heroes**

A young student is challenged by his teacher to complete an assignment to discover an unsung hero. During the project, the student learns about the heroic nature of his grandfather's past and is led to discover the true task, finding *The Hero Within*. *The Hero Within* is just one of the inspirational stories you will find within the walls of the Lowell Milken Center for Unsung Heroes in Fort Scott, Kansas. The LMC uses project-based learning to help students and educators discover, develop and communicate the stories of Unsung Heroes who have made a profound and positive impact on the course of history. By championing these Unsung Heroes, students, educators and communities discover their own power and responsibility to effect positive change in the world. Visit www.lowellmilkencenter.org to learn more.

Michael Berndt
AUTHOR

Michael Berndt, with over 15 years of teaching in both the elementary and secondary levels, has demonstrated his commitment to education by serving on a diverse level of building leadership positions including math lead teacher, refining curriculum with the Assessing Science Knowledge team, and even revising standards for his district's health curriculum. He has been recognized on the national level for his support in helping his school earn the prestigious Schools of Distinction Award for their dynamic efforts to raise mathematic scores. Berndt centers his philosophy on creating relationships in the classroom and promoting a positive and safe environment that meets the needs of the individual learner. Specializing in cooperative learning in his classroom, Berndt engages his students in higher-level thinking and a depth of knowledge. In 2012, Berndt became a national award winning teacher by being named the Milken Educator for the state of Kansas. In 2013, Berndt was selected as a Lowell Milken Center Fellow, where he collaborated with top educators, participating in a prestigious professional development opportunity with high standards of excellence focused on project-based learning.

Brad LeDuc
ILLUSTRATOR

Brad LeDuc, an artist and high school art teacher in Topeka, Kansas, grew up in a small town in the Midwest. It was here as a young boy that he found a passion for creating before going to school to become an educator. He has been instrumental in helping develop dynamic art programs at several schools while providing a rigor and expectation for his students that have helped them earn top honors at numerous regional and national art competitions. LeDuc strives to promote an environment in his classroom that both challenges and nourishes his students in discovering a visual voice they may not have otherwise found. In 2013, LeDuc became a national award winning teacher after being named the Milken Educator for the state of Kansas and the 2013 Distinguished Kansan for Education. In 2014, LeDuc was selected as a Lowell Milken Center Fellow, where he collaborated with top educators, participating in a prestigious professional development opportunity with high standards of excellence focused on project-based learning.

Lowell Milken Center
FOR *Unsung Heroes*

Discover   Create   Change

ISBN 978-0-9988266-0-8

1st Edition 2017

Unsung Heroes Projects
STEPS TO GET STARTED

Assemble Your Storytellers

Determine Your Unsung Hero

Select Your Project Outcome

 Performance

 Documentary

Gather In-Depth Research

 Exhibit

 Website

Outline Your Project

Brainstorm Your Thesis

Discover Your Unsung Hero

Primary Research

Research Trips
Interviews & Oral Histories

Create a Project That Tells Your Unsung Hero's Story

Enter the Discovery Award

Share Your Story With Your School, Community, and the World

To access LMC's project-based learning guide and start an Unsung Hero project, visit:

www.LowellMilkenCenter.org

CPSIA information can be obtained
at www.ICGtesting.com
Printed in the USA
LVHW01n2245150218
566829LV00002B/4/P